W9-AWN-823

To Maureen Cannon, that's Whooooo.
—M.S.

A hoot and a holler
for Sammy and Annie.
—J.S.

Text copyright © 2007 by Mary Serfozo
Illustrations copyright © 2007 by Jeffrey Scherer
All rights reserved.
Published in the United States by Random House Children's Books, a division of Random House, Inc., New York.
RANDOM HOUSE and colophon are registered trademarks of Random House, Inc.
www.randomhouse.com/kids
Educators and librarians, for a variety of teaching tools, visit us at www.randomhouse.com/teachers
Library of Congress Cataloging-in-Publication Data
Serfozo, Mary.
Whooo's there? / by Mary Serfozo ; illustrated by Jeffrey Scherer. — 1st ed.
p.   cm.
SUMMARY: An inquisitive owl keeps track of the comings and goings
of woodland creatures all night long.
ISBN 978-0-375-84050-0 (trade) — ISBN 978-0-375-94050-7 (lib. bdg.)
[1. Owls—Fiction. 2. Forest animals—Fiction. 3. Stories in rhyme.]
I. Scherer, Jeffrey, ill. II. Title. III. Title: Who's there? IV. Title:
Whooo is there? V. Title: Who is there?
PZ8.3.S4688Whs 2007
[E]—dc22
2006014438
PRINTED IN CHINA
10 9 8 7 6 5 4 3 2 1
First Edition

Whooo's there?

By Mary Serfozo • Illustrated by Jeffrey Scherer

Random House 🏠 New York

Quiet crept into
the dark forest deep.
Wrapped in the hush,
everyone seemed asleep.
Until . . .

"**Whooo's** there?" said Old Owl.
"Who said 'eee eee eee eee'?"

"I did," said Cricket.

"It's music to me."

"*Whooo!*" said Old Owl.
"Who has turned on the light?"
Fireflies glowed, a bright show
in the night.

"Whooo!" said Old Owl.

"Who pads softly like that?"

"Meeeow," said the cat.

"Anyone see a rat?"

"*Whooo!*" said Old Owl.

"Who tipped trash over there?"

"I did," Raccoon said.

"There's plenty to share."

Big yellow moon then comes peeking to see
what all the fuss in the forest could be.

"Whooo!" said Old Owl.

"Who's all snuffle and bark?"

Sniff, sniff. "It's Dog,

chasing Cat in the dark."

"*Whooo!*" said Old Owl.

"Who's that hopping on by?"

"*Ribbit,*" said Frog.

"*Ribbit, ribbit—goodbye!*"

"Whewwww!" said Old Owl.

"I know Skunk's down below!

Hi and goodbye, Skunk.

Now hurry! Please go!"

"**Whooo's** there?" said Old Owl.

"Who can scurry like that?"

"It's Rat," said the rat,

"and still faster than Cat."

Moonlight comes slipping between the tall trees.

Deep shadows stir as leaves lift in the breeze.

"Whooo!" said Old Owl.

"Who's that out on the prowl?"

"Ow-ooooo!" yowled Coyote.

"I prowl with a howl!"

"*Whooo!*" said Old Owl.

"Who swoops through the night sky?"

"Bats heading home,

but we can't stop—we're shy."

Tired old Moon is beginning to fade.

Stillness drifts back through the deep forest glade.

A lullaby hush

finds its way to the tree,

where somebody's sleeping now. . . .

Whooo can it be?